Sandra Magsamen is a world-renowned artist, author, and designer whose products and ideas have touched millions of lives. Her books and stories are a heartfelt reminder that it's the people and moments in our lives that make life so wonderful!

Big heartfelt thanks to Karen Botti and Hannah Magsamen Barry. Their creativity and generous spirits are unique and valued gifts to me and the work we create in the studio.

Published by Sourcebooks Jabberwocky, an imprint of Sourcebooks, Inc.
P.O. Box 4410, Naperville, Illinois 60567-4410
(630) 961-3900
Fax: (630) 961-2168
sourcebooks.com

Library of Congress Cataloging-in-Publication Data is on file with the publisher.

Source of Production: Leo Paper, Heshan City, Guangdong Province, China
Date of Production: September 2017
Run Number: 5010256

Printed and bound in China.
LEO 10 9 8 7 6 5 4 3 2 1

Have you ever felt like you're just too **small** to do important stuff in the world at all?

Well, take a closer look, and then you'll see how the **smallest** of things are as **mighty** as can be!

This itty-bitty **seed** doesn't seem so great at first, but when you plant it in the ground, you can see a flower **burst!**

Bees are tiny, too, but they travel far and wide to gather lots of nectar and **zip** back to their hive!

Ants build mini mazes that are hidden in the earth. They can **lift** enormous objects just a few days after birth!

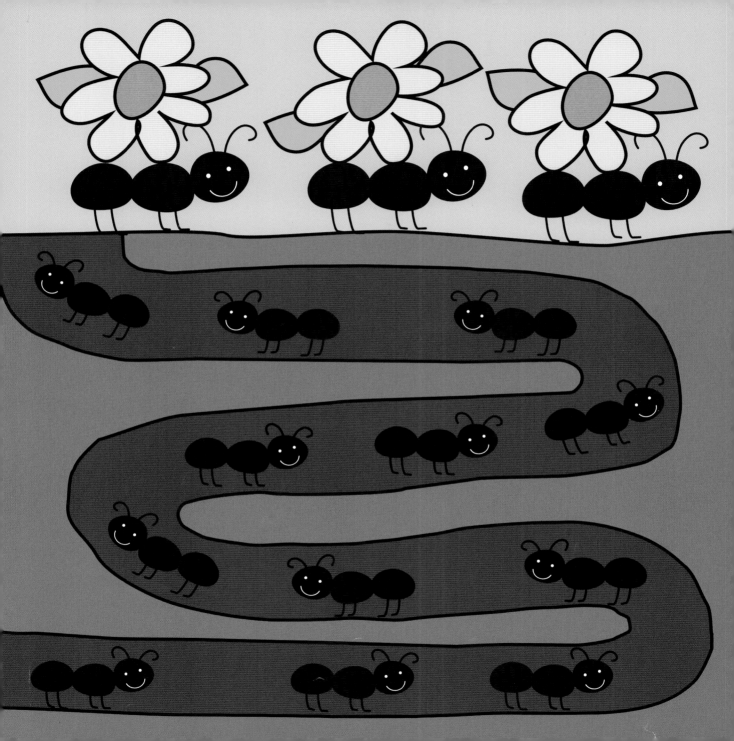

Teeny-weeny **hummingbirds** flutter low and high. Their wings beat super fast as they **hum** across the sky!

This little **butterfly** is indeed a pretty sight, but when it joins its friends they'll take a **spectacular** flight!

Worms

wiggle round and round. These guys are tiny **bulldozers,** moving mountains of soil around!

Are you starting to see all the **bigness of small?** Things that are little can be the **mightiest** of all.

You might not have

ama

+too!

incre

things only

known it, but you're

zing

There are

dible

you can do!

You can have a feeling that seems **little** at the start, but you can help the world if you believe with all your **heart!**

When you explore ideas and talents that are your very own, they'll be your **superpowers** now and when you've grown!

You see, small can be **BIG** in so many ways. It's just by being **YOU** that you'll always amaze!

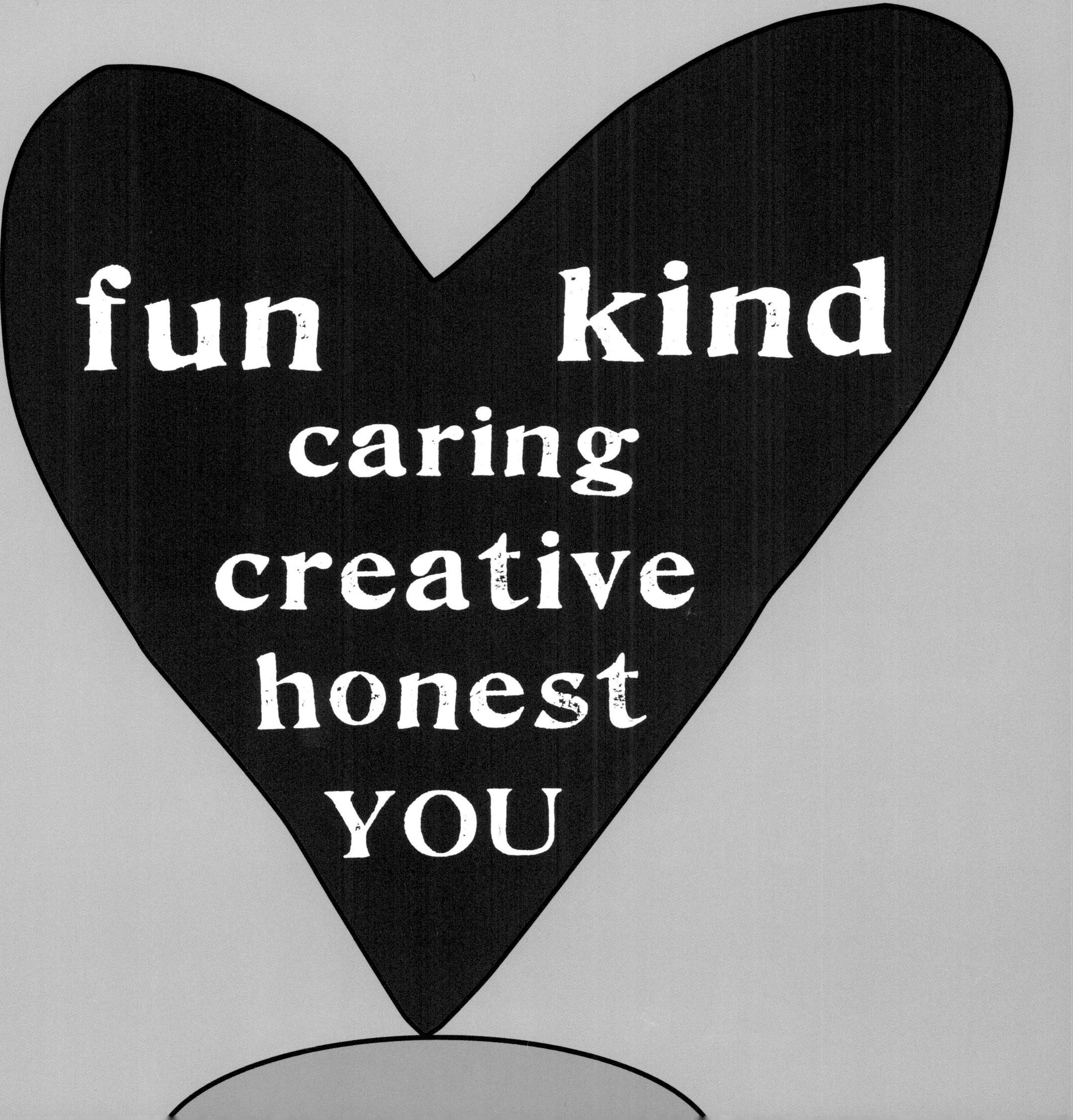
fun
kind
caring
creative
honest
YOU

So if you ever think "I can't" because you're just too **small...** now you know you **can** because you're **not so small at all!**

BIG FACTS
about not so small things

seeds

The smallest seed in the world is from an orchid that grows in the tropical rainforest. This seed is smaller than a dust particle!

The biggest seed in the world is from a palm tree called the coco-de-mer palm. It can grow up to twelve inches long and weigh more than forty pounds!

bees

Did you know that there are about 20,000 different types of bees in the world? And they're not all black and yellow—some of them are blue! The Blue Orchard Bee is used as a pollinator of sweet cherries and almonds.

Bees pollinate about 75% of the fruits and vegetables we eat. Without bees, we wouldn't have apples, oranges, watermelons, grapes, and a whole bunch of other food.

There are more than 10,000 known species of ants in the world! The only continent where they are not found is ANT-arctica.

The ant is actually one of the world's strongest creatures! Some species can carry up to fifty times their own weight. That would be about the same as an adult carrying a van down your street!

ants

hummingbirds

A hummingbird can fly nonstop for 500 miles—or about 20 hours—during migration season. Most hummingbirds migrate during the winter, and can survive in -4°F weather!

Hummingbirds are the only birds that can fly backwards. They can also hover in midair by flapping their wings up to 80 times per second, and can fly up to 26 miles per hour. That's faster than the average person can run!